Whale Shines

AN ARTISTIC TALE

FIONA ROBINSON

Abrams Books for Young Readers ★ New York

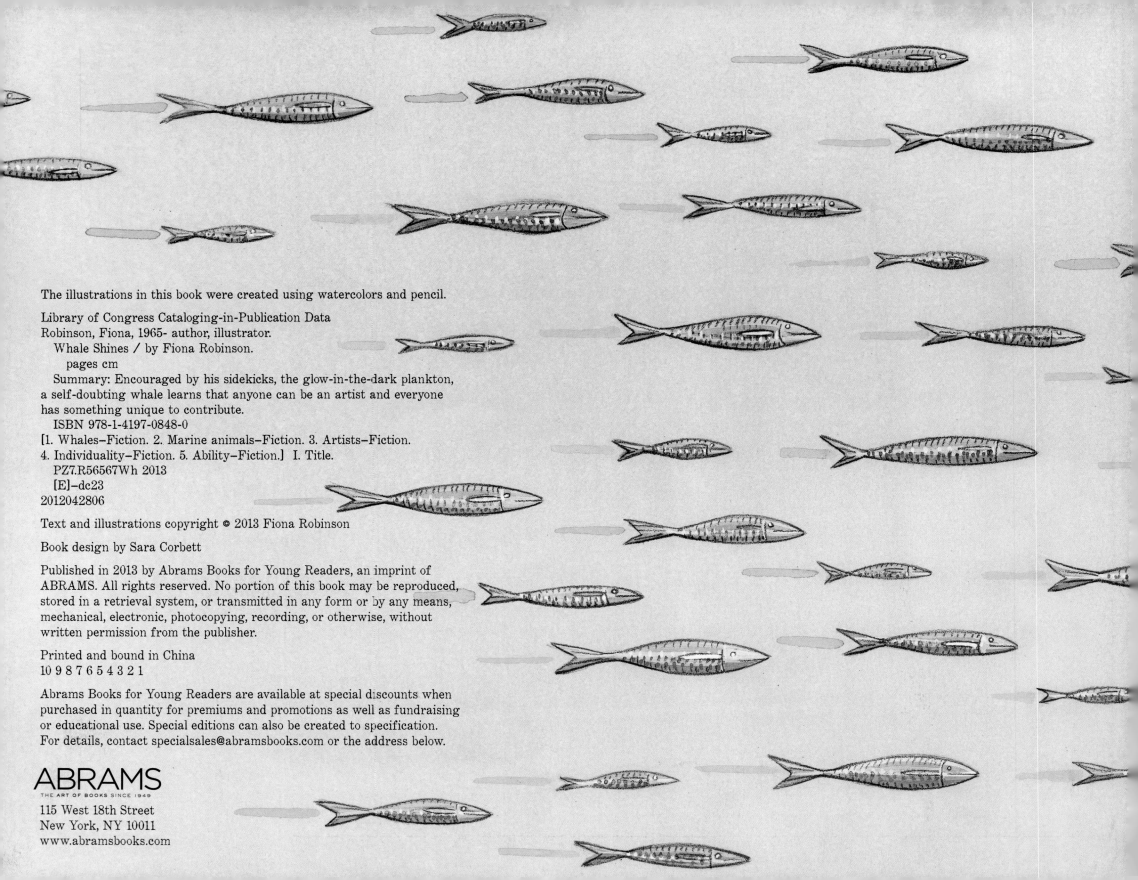

The illustrations in this book were created using watercolors and pencil.

Library of Congress Cataloging-in-Publication Data
Robinson, Fiona, 1965- author, illustrator.
   Whale Shines / by Fiona Robinson.
      pages cm
   Summary: Encouraged by his sidekicks, the glow-in-the-dark plankton,
a self-doubting whale learns that anyone can be an artist and everyone
has something unique to contribute.
   ISBN 978-1-4197-0848-0
[1. Whales–Fiction. 2. Marine animals–Fiction. 3. Artists–Fiction.
4. Individuality–Fiction. 5. Ability–Fiction.] I. Title.
   PZ7.R56567Wh 2013
   [E]–dc23
2012042806

Text and illustrations copyright © 2013 Fiona Robinson

Book design by Sara Corbett

Printed and bound in China
10 9 8 7 6 5 4 3 2 1

Abrams Books for Young Readers are available at special discounts when
purchased in quantity for premiums and promotions as well as fundraising
or educational use. Special editions can also be created to specification.
For details, contact specialsales@abramsbooks.com or the address below.

ABRAMS
THE ART OF BOOKS SINCE 1949
115 West 18th Street
New York, NY 10011
www.abramsbooks.com

FOR
PERRIN TAMAR FORNATALE

Once upon a tide . . .

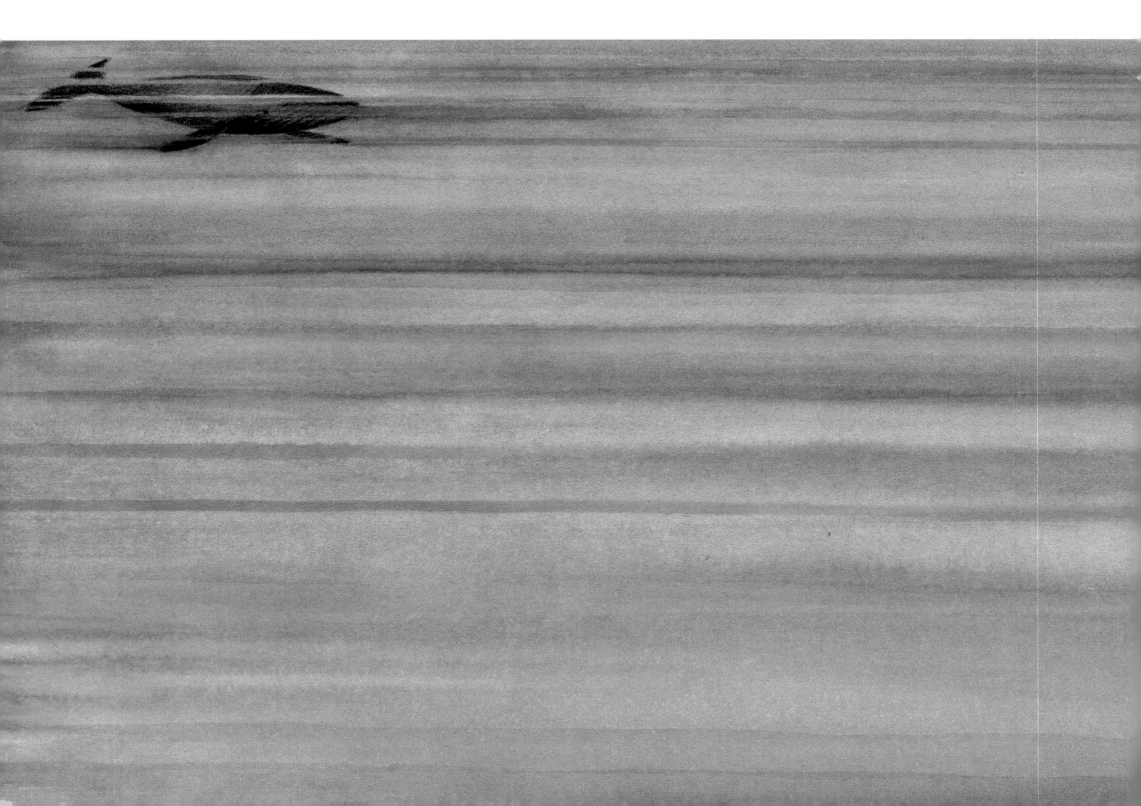

. . . a whale came with a message.

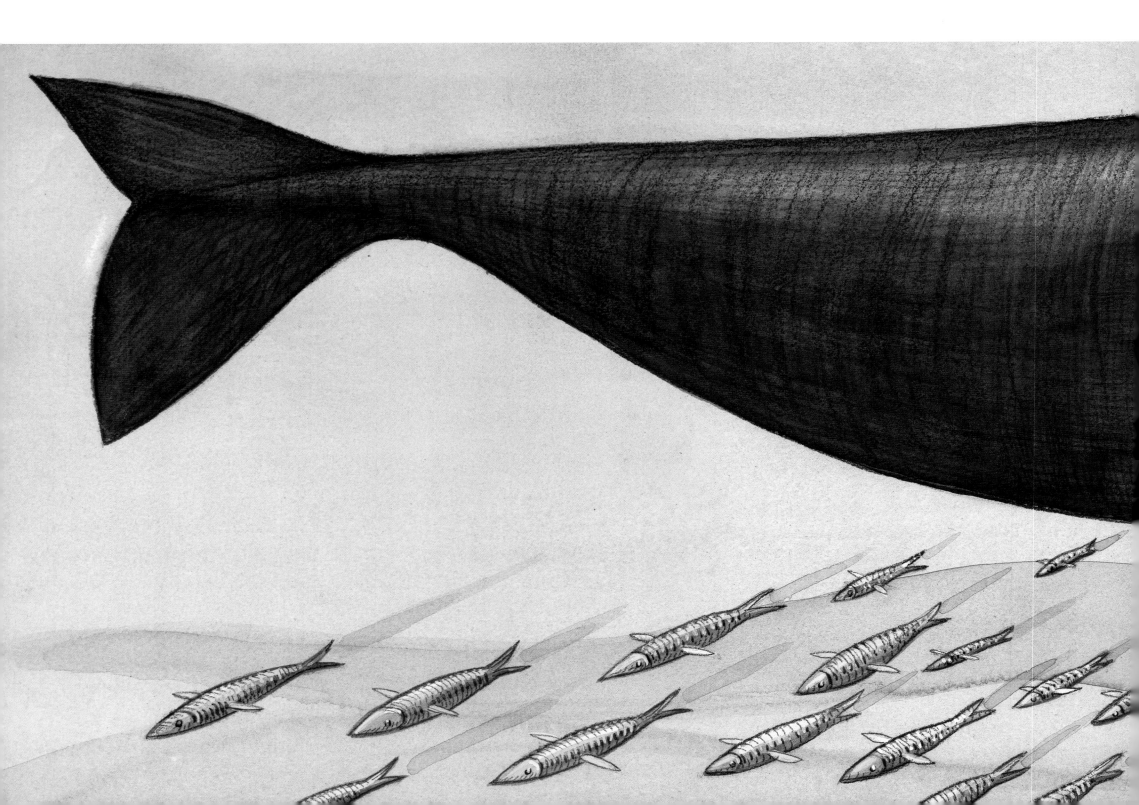

The whale slowed down as he passed the hammerhead shark. Hammerhead was busy creating sculptures from shipwrecks.

RT SHOW
Will you be ready
in time for the art show,
Hammerhead?
Of course, Whale!
But I can't stop to chat.
Hmm, I think I'll drape
these glass fishing floats
over the anchor. They'll look
terrific at the art show!

He paused by the eel and the wrasse. Eel was wriggling in the sand, forming patterns.

Wrasse was playfully changing his color to match his surroundings.

Then he passed by the studio of the octopus, the cuttlefish, and the giant squid. They barely noticed him.

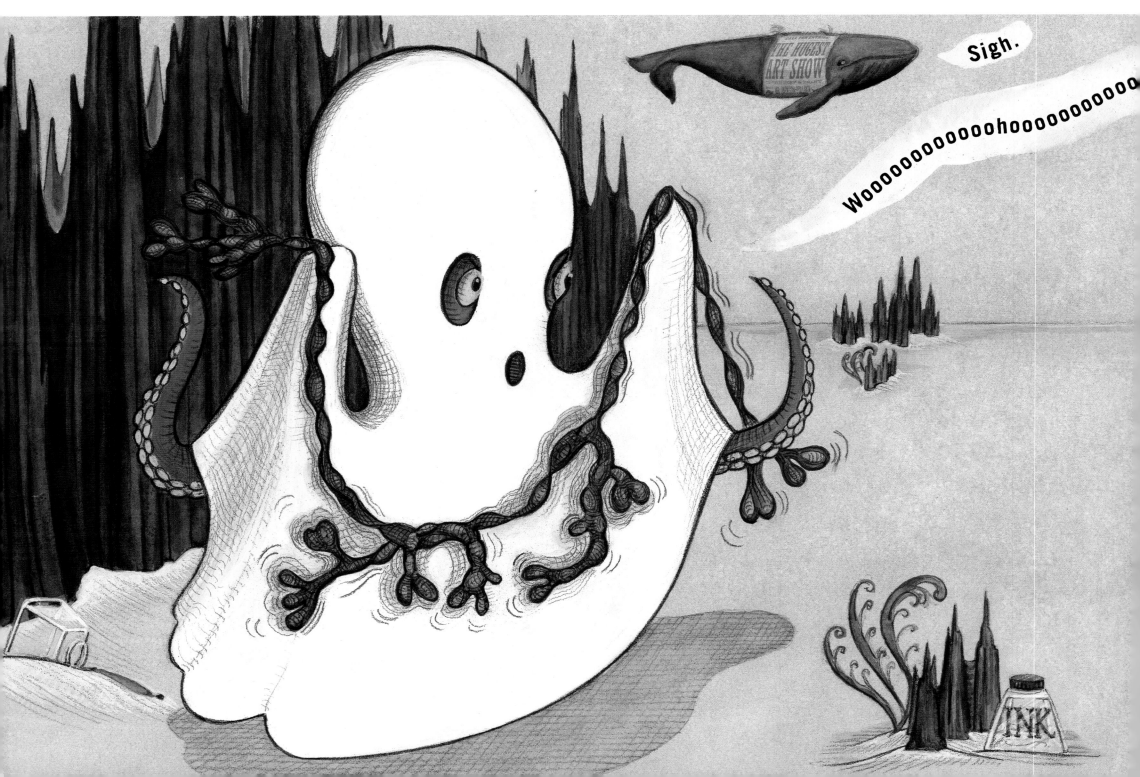

They were absorbed in trying to scare one another into producing ink for their paintings.

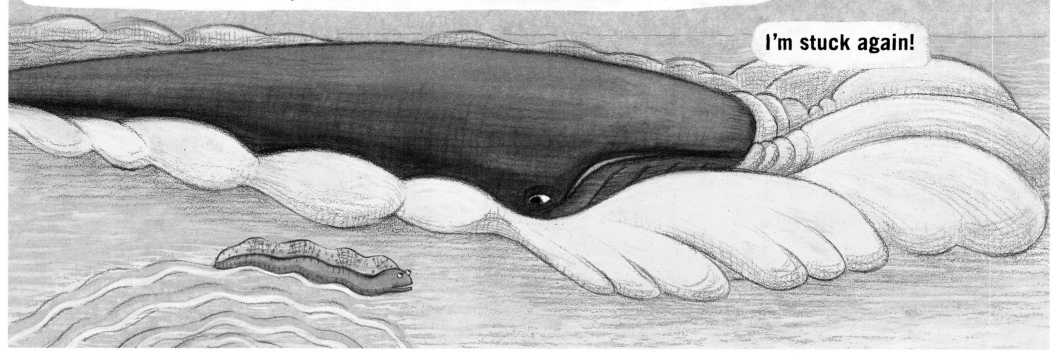

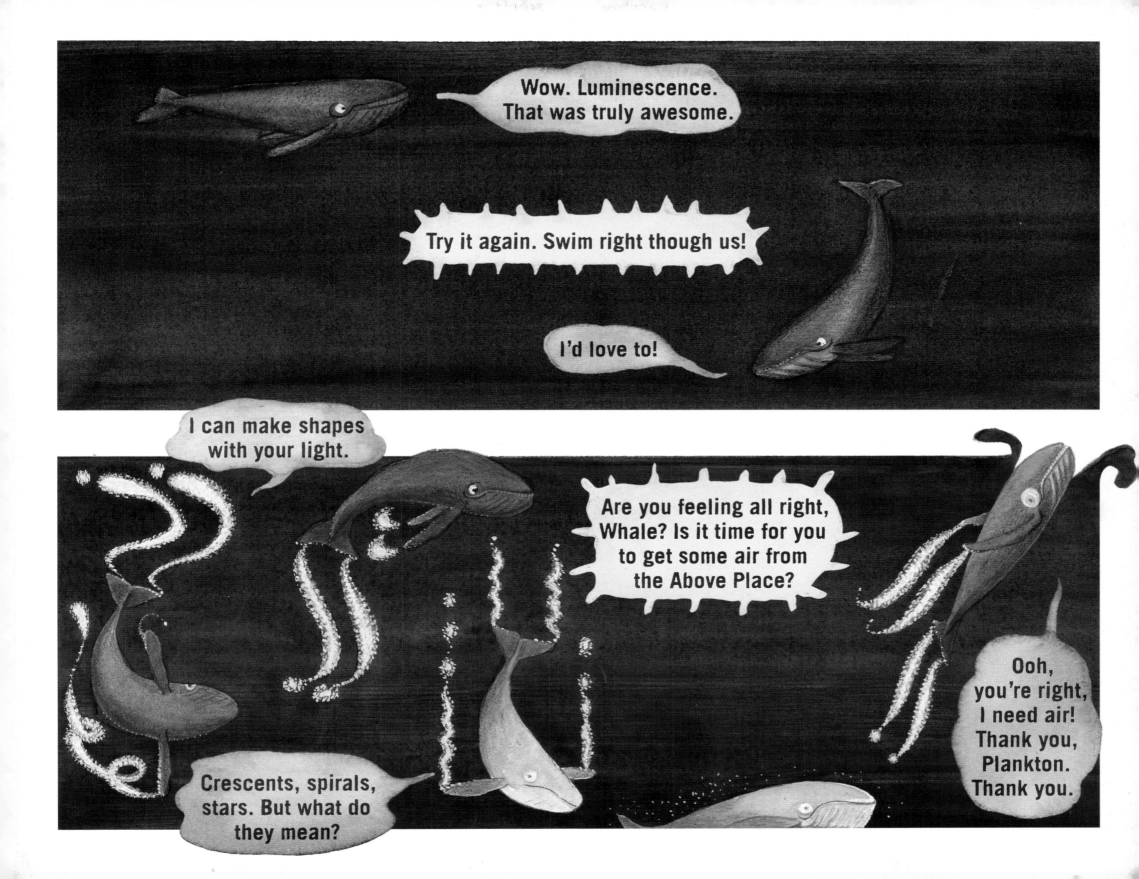

Whale shot to the surface, gasping for air. Then he basked in the glow of the moon and watched the starry night.

"Such a shame the other sea creatures never get to see what I see," he said.

"They only get to see the sky through a dulling veil of water."
All of a sudden Whale had an idea. He was going to do a painting after all.
He went to find the plankton.

Later that week, the art show took place. Mr. Jackson Pollock, a fish and the show's curator, was there to congratulate the exhibitors on their creations.

Whale rose up into the dark water and painted his picture. His giant body was his paintbrush, the plankton his paint, the ocean his canvas.

As he slowed, the stars and moon disappeared again and all the creatures raced forward to applaud him. He bowed.

Later . . .